Think Big!

Robert Munsch

illustrated by
Dave Whamond

Scholastic Canada Ltd.
Toronto New York London Auckland Sydney
Mexico City New Delhi Hong Kong Buenos Aires

One day Jamaal woke up early and said, "I've had it. My room is too small. I am the biggest kid, and I have the smallest room."

He went down to the breakfast table
and said, "Mom, my little brother has a
bigger room than I do. My littlest brother
has a room with a bunk bed, and it's bigger
than my room. I am the biggest kid, and I
should have the biggest room."

"Well, I am sorry, Jamaal," said his
mother, "but that's the way it is."

"Rats," said Jamaal.

So Jamaal went to see his father. He said, "Dad, I am the biggest kid in this family and I have the smallest room. My little brother has a bigger room than mine and my littlest brother even has bunk beds. It's not fair!"

"Now, Jamaal," said his father, "that's the way it is."

"Rats," said Jamaal.

Jamaal walked around all day in a terrible mood. Finally, about midnight, when everybody was asleep, he decided he was going to do something.

So he very quietly went down to the garage and got all his dad's tools. He brought them back upstairs and started to work.

He moved one wall way over to the right.

He moved one wall way over to the left.

He pushed the ceiling up.

He put a hot tub in one corner.
He put a bunk bed in the other corner.
He put an enormous stereo system by one wall.

He put up a big TV, looked around,
and said, "That's fine."
And then he went to sleep.

The first people to wake up the next morning were his mom and dad, and they realized that they were sleeping in a closet. "WHAT'S GOING ON?" they yelled.

Jamaal's littlest brother woke up and bumped his head on the ceiling when he sat up. He went out in the hall and said, "WHAT'S GOING ON?"

Jamaal's little brother woke up and his feet were sticking out the window. He ran out into the hall and yelled, "HEY, WHAT'S GOING ON?"

They all ran to Jamaal's bedroom. Jamaal was sitting in his hot tub and drinking orange juice while he watched his enormous TV.

"Hey, what's this?" said his father. "Where did you get this room?"

"Yeah," said his little brother.
"This room is too big."
"I made it all myself," said
Jamaal. "Pretty nice, huh?"

"This is terrible," said his littlest brother. "I'm going to put you in the garage."

"No," said his little brother, "I'm going to put you in the garbage can."

"This is horrible," said his mother. "Our bedroom is the size of a closet."

Jamaal's father looked around and said,
"Huuuuummmm. Nice job on the hot tub, Jamaal."
"Thank you," said Jamaal.
"Nice job on that TV."
"Thank you," said Jamaal.

"And nice job on the stereo."
"Thank you," said Jamaal.

"You know what?" said his dad. "You can keep this room. All you have to do is make us rooms just as nice."

"No problem," said Jamaal.

To Jamaal Dewberry, Fort Sill, Oklahoma
— R.M.

To my son, Zac — the builder with big ideas!
— D.W.

Scholastic Canada Ltd.
604 King Street West, Toronto, Ontario M5V 1E1, Canada

Scholastic Inc.
557 Broadway, New York, NY 10012, USA

Scholastic Australia Pty Limited
PO Box 579, Gosford, NSW 2250, Australia

Scholastic New Zealand Limited
Private Bag 94407, Botany, Manukau 2163, New Zealand

Scholastic Children's Books
Euston House, 24 Eversholt Street, London NW1 1DB, UK

www.scholastic.ca

These illustrations were done in a traditional crowquill pen, brush and ink,
followed by watercolours. The art was scanned and enhanced digitally.
The type is set in 20 point New Caledonia LT Std.

Library and Archives Canada Cataloguing in Publication

Title: Think big! / Robert Munsch ; illustrated by Dave Whamond.
Names: Munsch, Robert N., 1945- author. | Whamond, Dave, illustrator.
Description: Published simultaneously in hardcover by North Winds Press.
Identifiers: Canadiana 20200287087 | ISBN 9781443182980 (softcover)
Classification: LCC PS8576.U575 T45 2021b | DDC jC813/.54—dc23

7 6 5 4 3 2   Printed in China 62   22 23 24 25 26

FSC
MIX
Paper from
responsible sources
FSC® C020056